PAVEL AND THE TREE ARMY

This **PJ BOOK** belongs to

_____

_____

pj Library®

JEWISH BEDTIME STORIES and SONGS

For my dear friend Sue Brown, who knows all my best stories. —H.S.H.

For my mother and father —E.V.

KAR-BEN PUBLISHING, INC.
A division of Lerner Publishing Group, Inc.
241 First Avenue North
Minneapolis, MN 55401 USA
1-800-4-KARBEN

Website address: www.karben.com

Main body text set in Optima. Typeface provided by Adobe Systems.

Library of Congress Cataloging-in-Publication Data

Names: Hyde, Heidi Smith, author. | Vavouri, Elisa, illustrator.
Title: Pavel and the tree army / by Heidi Smith Hyde ; Illustrated by Elisa Vavouri.
Description: Minneapolis : Kar-Ben Publishing, [2019] | Series: Kar-Ben favorites |
    Summary: Planting trees and doing other environmental projects for the Civilian
    Conservation Corps, Russian immigrants Pavel and Anatoly are happy to find
    employment during the Great Despression, but when other workers accuse them of
    not being "real Americans," Pavel and Anatoly learn the words to the Star Spangled
    Banner, newly designated by Congress as the national anthem.
Identifiers: LCCN 2018000274| ISBN 9781512444469 (lb : alk. paper) |
    ISBN 9781512444476 (pb : alk. paper)
Subjects: LCSH: Civilian Conservation Corps (U.S.)—Juvenile fiction. | CYAC: Civilian
    Conservation Corps (U.S.)—Fiction. | Immigrants—Fiction. | Depressions—1929—
    Fiction. | Jews—United States—Fiction. | Russian Americans—Fiction.
Classification: LCC PZ7.H9677 Pav 2019 | DDC [E]—dc23

LC record available at https://lccn.loc.gov/2018000274

PJ Library Edition ISBN 978-1-5415-6086-4

Manufactured in Hong Kong
1-46363-47468-7/17/2018

011928.4K1/B1334/A7

PAVEL
AND THE
TREE ARMY

Heidi Smith Hyde
illustrated by Elisa Vavouri

KAR-BEN
PUBLISHING

Pavel stood in line with hundreds of other hungry people,
hoping for a scrap of bread or a warm bowl of soup.
Times were hard. Pavel was scouring the city in search of
a job, but there were no jobs—especially for immigrants
whose English was not very good.

On Shabbat, the rabbi said to him, "Pavel, there is a new work program called the Civilian Conservation Corps. Young men like you are being paid to plant trees all over the country— in Virginia, Montana, Oklahoma . . ."

Pavel brightened. "I could plant trees for America!"

A month later Pavel arrived in Idaho—a dry, dusty land dotted with wheat fields and farmhouses. It couldn't have looked more different from New York City.

"Look, Pavel! No bread lines stretching around the block," said his friend Anatoly as they stepped off the train into a world of quiet.

Pavel gripped his satchel. "Will we really get three meals a day?" he marveled, thinking about the many nights he and his sisters had gone to bed hungry.

Anatoly nodded. "That's what they say. And with the money we earn, our families can eat too."

They made their way to the camp where the workers were living. Pavel met men from all over the country: Otis from Oklahoma, Wilbur from Kansas, Lester from Louisiana, Giovanni from Illinois, and Homer from Maine.

"You and your friend don't sound like you're from around here," sneered Otis, whose cot was next to Pavel's.

"Anatoly and I were born in Russia, but we are Americans now," said Pavel proudly.

"Y'all don't sound like Americans," drawled Lester.

"Don't mind them, Pavel," Anatoly whispered. "We are just as American as they are."

The workers piled into a truck and drove to a nearby field. "Welcome to the Civilian Conservation Corps!" said Sergeant Sterling. "For the next few months you will clear brush, plant young trees, and build roads and dams. Your job is to help make America beautiful."

"But I don't know how to plant trees," murmured Pavel.
"Don't worry, Pavel. We will learn," said Anatoly. Gazing at the
unfamiliar landscape, Pavel wondered if this vast, open space
would ever feel like home.

Grabbing picks and shovels, the men ventured
out into the field and set to work.

Together they dug . . .

And planted . . .

And packed . . .

And watered . . .

At the end of the day, Pavel gazed at their work. "We did it, Anatoly! We planted a whole forest of trees!" he exclaimed. Suddenly the land seemed a little less vast.

In the mess hall, Pavel feasted on chicken and mashed potatoes, and for dessert he helped himself to a big slice of apple pie.

"This tastes almost as good as my mama's Shabbat chicken," said Anatoly.

"And my mama's chicken cacciatore," said Giovanni with a grin. Giovanni had come to America from Italy.

Otis gave them a disdainful look. "You don't belong in the Civilian Conservation Corps. You're not *real* Americans. I bet you don't even know America's national anthem."

Pavel stared at him blankly.

Homer jumped in. "It's called 'The Star-Spangled Banner' and Congress just made it our national song."

"All real Americans can sing the national anthem," said Otis with a smirk. "Can you?"

Pavel and his friends exchanged worried glances.
"We don't know it, but we can learn it," said
Anatoly with determination.
"I'll teach you," whispered Homer.

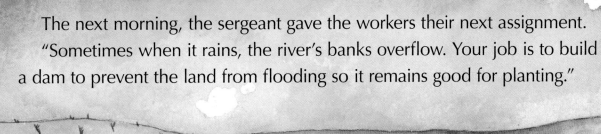

The next morning, the sergeant gave the workers their next assignment. "Sometimes when it rains, the river's banks overflow. Your job is to build a dam to prevent the land from flooding so it remains good for planting."

"But I don't know how to build a dam," Giovanni murmured.
"Don't worry, Giovanni," Pavel told him, patting him on the back.
"We will learn."

Together they dug trenches . . .

And cut timber . . .

And gathered rocks.

At night they camped on the bank of the river and
shared stories around the fire.

In the barracks, Pavel and his friends struggled to learn the words to "The Star-Spangled Banner." Homer helped them practice.

"These English words are too hard. I can't do it," said Anatoly.

"Maybe Otis is right. Maybe we're not real Americans," sighed Giovanni.

"We must keep trying," said Pavel. "If we can learn to build a dam, we can learn the national anthem."

On the last Friday of the month, the workers got their pay. "This will be enough to buy new shoes for my sisters—and a chicken for Shabbat dinner!" said Pavel.

That night, Otis and Lester went to the movies. Giovanni went dancing. Pavel and Anatoly rested from the hard week's work, singing Shabbat songs from home.

One summer morning Sergeant Sterling announced, "Next week we will have a Fourth of July picnic." The camp was abuzz with excitement.

"What is so special about the Fourth of July?" Pavel asked.
"It's Independence Day—the day we celebrate our freedom!" answered Wilbur. "It reminds us how lucky we are to be Americans."

On the Fourth
of July, the men put
away their tools and
celebrated the holiday.

Sergeant Sterling came over to Pavel and Anatoly.
"You and the others have helped make this land
beautiful. America is proud of you."

Pavel looked at him doubtfully. "Some of the men say we aren't real Americans because we were not born here," he said.

The sergeant thought for a moment. Then he pointed to the grove of young trees in the distance. "It will take time for the saplings you planted to take root, but they are now part of this land. And so are you."

That night, everyone gathered at the lake to sing the new national anthem and watch a fireworks display.

"Are you ready?" Pavel asked his friends.

"I think so," said Giovanni.

"We are!" said Anatoly firmly.

They stood at attention and put their hands over their hearts. In clear, confident voices, they joined in singing the "The Star-Spangled Banner" from beginning to end.

Everyone cheered as red, white, and blue fireworks exploded in the sky.

"I am . . . an American," whispered Pavel proudly.

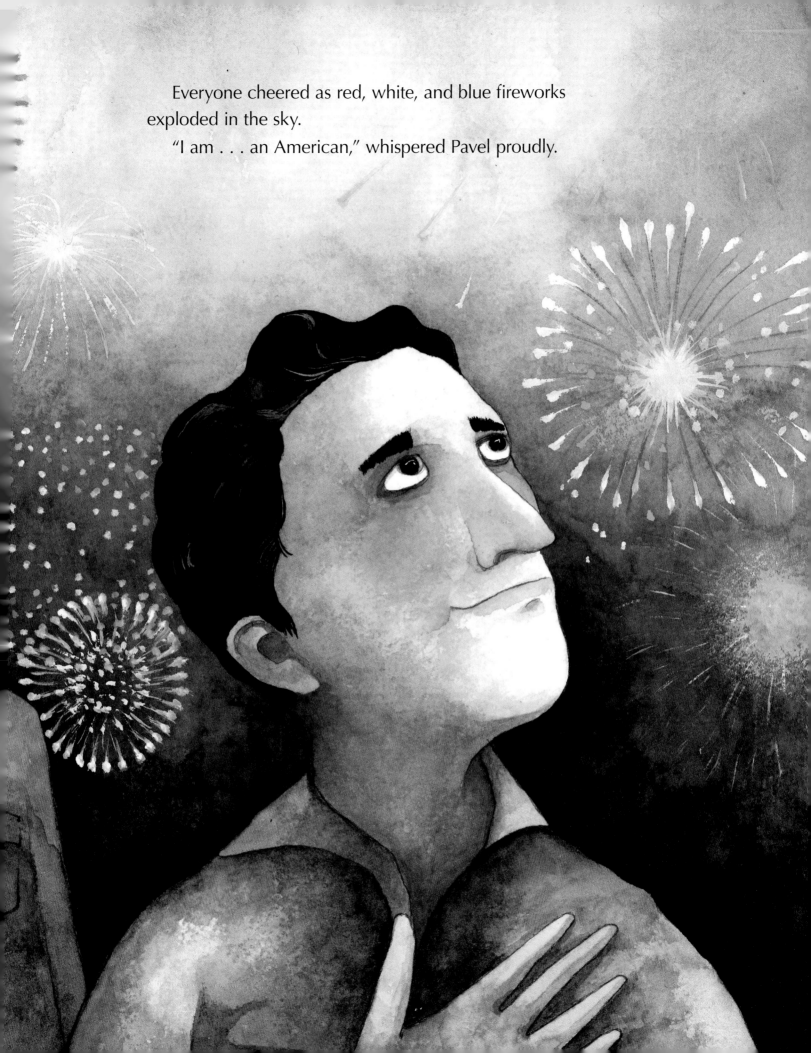

Author's Note

During the Great Depression in the 1930s, President Franklin Roosevelt established an important program known as the Civilian Conservation Corps. Known as "America's Tree Army," the Corps became President Roosevelt's most popular Depression-era initiative, providing jobs for thousands of young men, many of them poor, unemployed Jewish immigrants. Together they performed essential conservation projects across America, such as tree planting, trail construction, state park development, dam building, and more. Thanks to the efforts of the Corps, more than three billion trees were planted from Montana to South Carolina. These hardworking young men were responsible for much of the national park infrastructures we still enjoy today.

Civilian Conservation Corps members head out for a Jewish holiday celebration in St. Joe National Forest

According to researcher Naomi Sandweiss, the Jewish men who participated in the Corps explored unfamiliar parts of the country, shedding remnants of their immigrant selves, and for the first time embracing both their American and Jewish identities. Housed in tents or barracks supervised by the Department of War, these Depression-era Jewish immigrants created community and even celebrated Shabbat and Rosh Hashanah together.

Pavel and his friends learning to sing the national anthem in this story is also historically accurate. Francis Scott Key wrote a poem in 1814 about the British bombardment of Fort McHenry in Maryland during the War of 1812. That poem was later set to music and in 1931, during the years of the Corps, it became America's national anthem, "The Star-Spangled Banner."